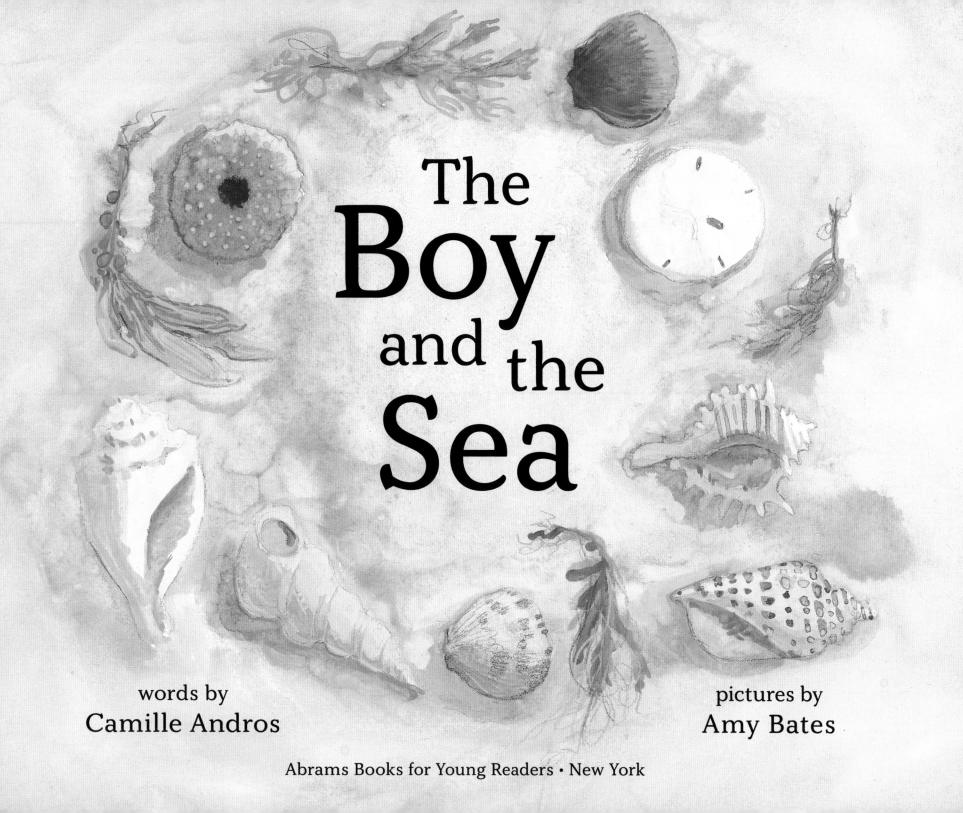

The Boy and the Sea

words by
Camille Andros

pictures by
Amy Bates

Abrams Books for Young Readers · New York

The art in this book was created with gouache, watercolor, and colored pencil.

Cataloging-in-Publication Data has been applied for
and may be obtained from the Library of Congress.

ISBN 978-1-4197-4940-7

Printed and bound in China
10 9 8 7 6 5 4 3 2 1

Abrams Books for Young Readers are available at special discounts when purchased in
quantity for premiums and promotions as well as fundraising or educational use.
Special editions can also be created to specification.
For details, contact specialsales@abramsbooks.com or the address below.

Abrams® is a registered trademark of Harry N. Abrams, Inc.

ABRAMS The Art of Books
195 Broadway, New York, NY 10007
abramsbooks.com

For the Sea, who whispered this story to me
—C.A.

To Chester
—A.B.

Once there was a boy
who lived by the sea.

The sea was old and wise.

The boy liked to listen to its whispers.

From time to time,
the sea was
dark and dangerous.

So was the boy.

Other times,
the sea was
tranquil and tender.

So was the boy.

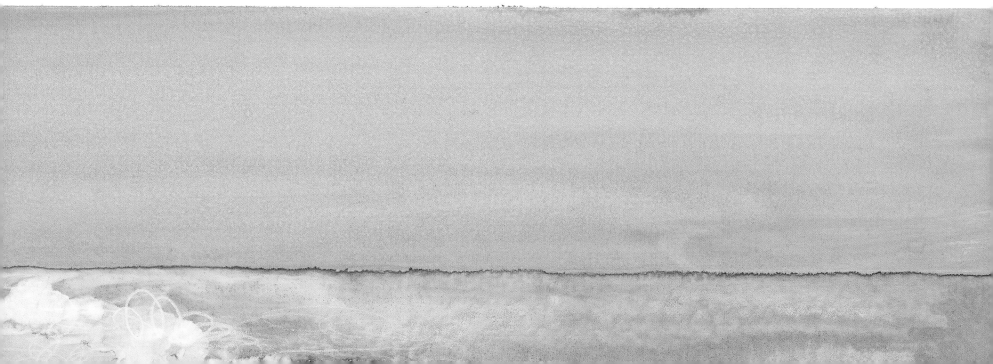

But, once in a while,

the sea felt

the pull of something more.

And the boy did, too.

The boy liked to think,
and often his thoughts
turned into questions.

Some of his questions
had answers . . .

but many did not.

So he returned to the waves and their whispers.

The boy sat
and he listened,
and he thought
he heard the sea say . . .

Dream.

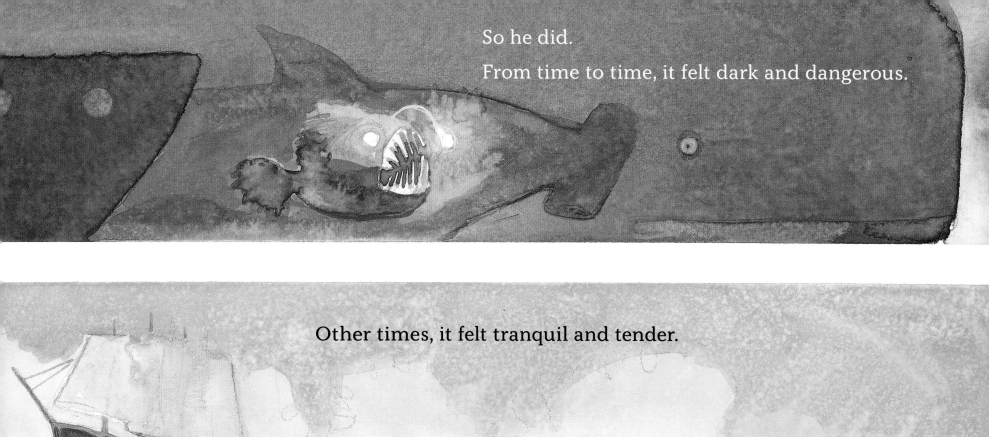

So he did.

From time to time, it felt dark and dangerous.

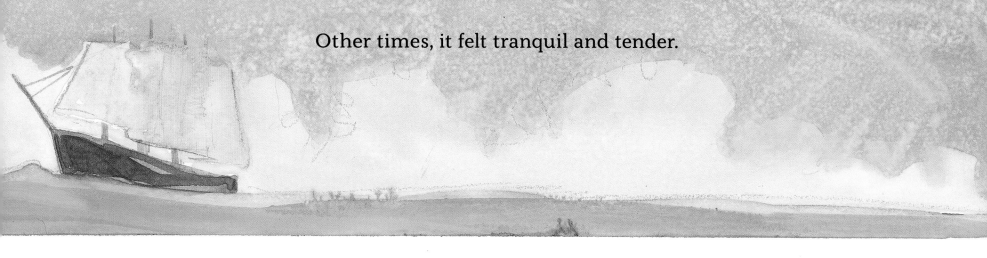

Other times, it felt tranquil and tender.

But, once in a while,
the boy felt the pull
of something more.

As the boy grew,
his questions became
more complicated.

Answers were fewer
and farther between.

So he returned to the waves
and their whispers.

The boy sat
and he listened,
and he thought he heard
the sea say . . .

Love.

So he did.

From time to time, it felt dark and dangerous.

Other times, it felt tranquil and tender.

But, once in a while,

the boy felt the pull of something more.

Then, the boy was grown.

He thought by being grown,
he'd finally know the answers
to his questions.

But he did not.

He only knew

more was answered in his asking.

So he returned to the waves and
their whispers and asked.

The boy sat
and he listened,
and he thought he heard the sea say . . .

From time to time, it felt dark and dangerous.

Other times, it felt tranquil and tender.

And, once in a while, the boy felt the pull of something more.

Once there was a boy who lived by the sea.

The boy was old and wise.

He liked to think,
and often his thoughts
turned into questions.

Some of his questions had answers, but many did not.

So the boy sat . . .

And he listened.